T0129686

Secrets
Beyond the
Whispers

Sophia Gayle D. Eutsey

WESTBOW
PRESS®
A DIVISION OF THOMAS NELSON
& ZONDERVAN

WestBow Press books may be ordered through booksellers or by contacting:

WestBow Press
A Division of Thomas Nelson & Zondervan
1663 Liberty Drive
Bloomington, IN 47403
www.westbowpress.com
1 (866) 928-1240

ISBN: 978-1-9736-8828-0 (sc)
ISBN: 978-1-9736-8829-7 (e)

Print information available on the last page.

WestBow Press rev. date: 04/03/2020

DEDICATION

THIS BOOK IS dedicated to my Wonderful family: My husband, our children, our siblings, other loved ones, and people who thought to read it: I always value one's good thought. I dedicate this book to individuals I find very dear to me, as well. Here's a few: My wonderful aunts, Ammie Medley and Annie Eutsey Carter. My dear mother-n-law, Polly M. Jones and her twin sister, Author M. White. My awesome cousins, Mr. and Mrs. Emel Eutsey Sr., Mr. and Mrs. George Kelley, Sharon Lea Eutsey, Rosie Eutsey Holloman, and Linda Eutsey McDuffie. Long-time friends, Katherine S. Warren, Angel H. Bryant, Ms. Daisy Gardner Lester, and Mr. Timothy Green. I love everybody, and I know God loves us more. Thanks to all who pray for me with positive thoughts. God Bless You!

TABLE OF CONTENTS

CHAPTER 1

Family Ties

"I WONDER WHAT'S taking Alvey so long; It's hot out here." Said a local residence, while waiting for her niece at a supermarket. "Hi Alvenia, what can I do for you?" Said a well-known store owner, moving quickly. The customer replied, "Some Almond Delight ice cream, please." "Alright, that'll be 3 dollars and fifty cents." "3 dollars are all I have sir." "No problem. Tell Jessica I said hi." "She's out in the car; I'll tell her. Bye!" "Can you walk faster, Alvey?!" "I'm walking fast as I could, Aunt Jessie; this ice cream is heavy. Here." "My, this is heavy." "I told you. It must've been the only size he had, too; You didn't give me enough money." "Please don't slam that door. It's bad enough the air conditioner is broken, and the heat has given me a headache." Said Alvenia's Aunt Jessica, wiping sweat off her face. "I'm not going to slam it. Mr. Montgomery said hi." "Did he?" "Yes." "Alright, let's go home." Said Aunt

Jessie, as she turned the key in the ignition of her two-tone, 'black and white' (1968 Ford Mustang).

Alvenia was named, 'Alvenia Hutchinson'. She had brown eyes and blond hair. During Spring '1977', she was age 17, 5ft 5 inches tall, and scrawny; weighing 108 lbs. She lived in (The Bronx New York) with her aunt who was named, 'Jessica Steward'. Jessica was 36 and single. She never married or had any children. However, she was raising Alvenia. She called her, Alvey. Alvenia's mother was Jessica's older sister, Carol Steward Hutchinson. Her father was Daniel Hutchinson. The couple met in 1953. At the time, Daniel was a young soldier in the US Army. Carol was a high school senior; They married soon after she graduated. Then in 1954, Carole enrolled at 'Albert Einstein College'. 4 years later she received a medical degree and became a nurse: They had Alvenia in 1959.

In 1961, Daniel Hutchison was killed in the Vietnam war. Then in 1962, Carol decided to become a military nurse: She enlisted in the US Air Force.

Her basic training was done at Fort Polk. {Vernon Parish, Louisiana}. After training was over, she was sent to Vietnam. Sadly, during the war in 1964, the beloved Carol died from a viral epidemic. Alvenia was 5 and that's when Jessica became her legal guardian.

When they got home that Friday evening, Jessica said," I forgot today was garbage pickup; move the trash can after you open the gate Alvey, and get those bags from the back seat." When they stepped onto the porch, she said," The door is jammed again. Here take this. There it is; It was really stuck. Give me that, I'm going to my room and lie down; bring me a bowl of ice cream after you're done putting away everything,

Alvey." "Yes ma'am." Said Alvenia, holding 2 bags of groceries. Jessica laid across her bed.

"This bed feels so good." Hurry with that ice cream, Alvey!" She shouted. "Okay, Aunt Jessie!"

Moments later, Alvenia gave Jessica the ice cream. "'This looks delicious." Said Jessica. "Can I have some, Aunt Jessie?" "I guess so, and when you're done with it, get those things out of my bathroom and put them in the wash." "Okay." Said Alvenia.

2 hours later, she knocked on Jessica's door and went in. "Aunt Jessie? Aunt Jessie', are you awake?" Jessica lifted her head from her pillow and said," I am now; what do you want?!" "Here's your laundry: I'm going outside now." "Do you ever get tired of that swing?" "No; I like listening to the birds chirp." "What time is it?" Jessica asked. "It's almost 4pm." "Don't forget you have to start dinner at 5." "I won't." Said Alvenia.

There was a London Plane tree in front of their home. A kind neighbor hung a swing on a branch 10 ft' high, for Alvenia. She loved that swing. She'll set down and take the flats off her feet, and she'd sing and swing as high as she could. Whenever there was a rainbow, she'd look at it and say: "You're beautiful, and I know you're still watching me, Mommy; I love you." After she'd swing a while, a 1975 mint green (Chevy Monza) drove up. It was Jessica's best friend, Betty Lou Nesbit, and her (70) year old aunt who was named, Francine Oneal Nesbit: They were African Americans. Betty Lou was 35, medium built, and very fair-skinned like her father. She and Jessica were LPN's. (Licensed Practice Nurses) They worked together at Elmhurst Hospital.

Francine was very small and had pecan complexion. Her hair was long and thick with specks of grey: a woman of grace and intelligence. She was born in The Bronx New York in 1915: an only child to Franklin and Harriet O'Neal. During the great depression, Francine was a young teenager; and life for the O'neal's was very hard. Franklin worked 2 jobs to support his family. He'd always say," I don't want my wife and daughter to lack for anything: I'll work 3 jobs if I have to." And he worked every Monday through Friday at an apple grove. On weekend nights he waited tables at the Harlem Savoy Ballroom. Harriett was a loving wife, mother, and homemaker. She always made sure Francine was well-groomed before she went anywhere. She instilled in her to focus on attaining a good education, also.

Francine graduated from 'Theodore Roosevelt High' in 1933, then immediately enrolled at New York City College. There is where she earned a degree in education. Thereafter she taught Math at the local high school. By 1944, she'd become an Activist and an Educator. While campaigning in 1946, she met an amazing man named Rudolph Nesbit. He was an accountant for a lumber company, and an Activist, too; They married in 1948, but never had any children. However, Rudolph had 1 brother who was named, Paul: He was a widow, and had one child. He died when the child was 10. After he died, Rudolph and Francine took full custody of his child. That child was Betty Lou.

When they drove up at Jessica's, Betty Lou, got out. "I'll only be a minute, Aunt Fran." She said. Francine watched her go inside, then looked at Alvenia. "Hi Alvenia!" She said. Alvenia kept swinging and said, "Hi Mrs. Francine!" "Come here Alvenia!" Alvenia stopped the swing, put on her flats, then jogged to Betty Lou's car. Francine noticed the old Bohemian maxi dress and flats she had on. After she'd reached the car, Francine asked, "How are you doing?" "I'm doing good, ma'am." "Did you go to school today?" "Yes." Alvenia answered, bashfully. "How was it?" Francine asked. "I guess it was okay." "Why you guess it was okay?" Alvenia's head was down. Francine said, "Look at me Alvenia: why do you guess it was ok?" "Ma'am, those kids at my school aren't very nice to me." "What do they do to you?" "They call me names and say I look like a rag doll; because I wear old clothes." "Do you have any friends?" "I had one; She moved a long time ago." Betty Lou walked out. Francine hurried and said, "Alvenia, when you get a chance, go out back to that path and come see me; and let that be our secret." "Yes, ma'am." Said Alvenia, with a smile. "Hi Alvey!" Said Betty Lou, walking fast to the car. "Hi Miss Betty! Bye Mrs. Francine." "Bye, Sweetie."

After Betty Lou got in and started the car, she asked, "What was Alvey talking about?" "She came over to say hi; She's a sweet girl." "Yes, she is Aunt Fran; I don't know why Jessica won't have her wear better clothes and do something to her hair. But so much about them, I need to get you home and situated; I have a dinner date this evening."

Francine became quiet. After a moment Betty Lou said," Are you okay, Aunt Fran; I hope you're not upset about me going out." No, it's that doctor's office. It always makes me restless, and I'm ready to get home and relax. So, don't worry about me, go on your date and enjoy yourself." Said Francine, holding her head slightly down. Betty Lou quickly said" Oh, I'm definitely going to enjoy myself."

Monday evening 3 days later, Jessica picked up Alvenia from school (August Martin High), took her home, then left. Alvenia knew she was meeting Betty Lou. So, she baked cookies while she did her chores. After they were done, she put them in a bowl and hurried out back to visit, Francine. There was a wooded area about 285 ft between their homes. Alvenia jogged through those woods all the way there. Francine's home was fairly nice, but comfortable. She had a private entrance on the side. Alvenia stepped onto the porch, then peek through the window. She saw Francine sitting on her bed and watching tv. She had on a sky blue and white (Sweet dress) with a matching (slinky scarf) and (house slippers). It was her favorite home attire; She had it in many different colors. Alvenia knocked. "Yes!" Said Francine. "It's Alvenia, ma'am." Francine stood up, grabbed her walker, then went and opened the door.

"Hello, ma'am." Said Alvenia, smiling. "Hi Alvenia; come in and have a seat." Alvenia set in Francine's rocker recliner. "You sound like you've been running, Dear." "I have, I want to get back before my aunt gets home." "Alright, but rest a minute. What happened to your shoe?" "That just happened while I was running through the woods." "Be careful going through those woods; It might be snakes and who knows what else is out there." "I know, ma'am."

"What's that in your hand?" Francine asked, curious. Alvenia uncovered the bowl and gave it to her. "It's some cookies I baked for you." "They smell good; look tasty, too. Yum, they are good. Did Jessica teach you how to bake?" Francine asked, after tasting one of the cookies. Alvenia said, "No, ma'am; She could only pour herself a bowl of cereal." Francine was tickled. Alvenia went on and said, "I learned from a lady I watch on tv." "Are you talking about 'Julia Child', the French chef?" "Yes ma'am, that's her!" Alvenia answered, excitedly. "Julia's been on tv a while: I used to watch her." "Really, ma'am?" "Yes, and she does have good recipes: In French and American. I have a few of her books; You can have one if you like." "Can I, ma'am?!" Francine smiled before saying: "Sure you can; They're right there on the chest." "Thanks Miss Francine." "You're welcome, Sweetie." "I better go now." Francine pointed at her night-stand as she said, "Wait, I have another book I want to give you; It's on my nightstand, the second from the top." Alvenia took the books, then Francine walked her to the door. "Be careful walking through those bushes." "Okay bye!"

CHAPTER 2

School Girl Days

ALVENIA GOT HOME 40 minutes before Jessica. "I'm home Alvey!" "I'm in the kitchen, Aunt Jessie!" Jessica went to the kitchen. "Why haven't you finished dinner?" She asked. "It's done; I'm putting away some things." "What is that smell like cake or something?" "It must be the cinnamon: I put some in the yams before I accidentally dropped it." "Be careful Alvey, we don't have money to waste; I surely don't, and yours about to stop coming. I'm going to the bathroom, go ahead and make my plate."

Moments later, Jessica returned to the kitchen and set down. "I thought my bladder was going to explode: what's for dinner, I'm hungry." Alvenia put her plate on the table. "Chicken again Alvey?!" She said, Yelling. "You don't like leftovers Aunt Jessie, and chicken is the only meat we have." Alvenia said, nervously. "Why didn't you tell me; I would've gone by the store today." "I don't know, Aunt Jessie." "Well I'm glad you cooked yams;

We haven't had any in a while, and the beans taste good, too." "Yeah, they do. I love green beans." Said Alvena. Jessica started eating then said," Pour me some coke on ice." "Yes ma'am." The soda was in the cabinet under the sink. When Alvenia bent to get it, she saw a cookie she'd dropped earlier. She picked it up and tossed it between the sink and the stove: She didn't want Jessica to know she'd baked them without her permission. She finally gave her the soda and set down.

Then after eating her first spoonful, she said," Aunt Jessie, what happened to Miss Francine?" "She was in a car accident; that was a long time ago." "Was she driving?" "Back then she had a husband, he was driving." "Did anything happen to him?" "Yes, he got hurt pretty bad." Alvenia went on and said," That must've been awful; who took care of them?" "Betty Lou had just graduated from high school; She decided to stay there and help." "Did you know Miss Betty then?" "Yes, and what's with all the questions Alvey?!" Alvenia fidget from Jessica's reaction. She replied, "I was just asking." "You've asked enough! Finish your dinner."

"We're taking our senior pictures next week." "Oh Really?" "Yes, and I was wondering if I can get something new to wear?" "I bought you a few things a couple of months ago Alvey! You need to learn how to fix yourself up better! We have bills to pay and they're not cheap!" Jessica said, talking loudly." "Will you do my hair?" "I'll see what I can do to it." "Thank you, Aunt Jessie!" "There's no need to get all excited. I'm going to my room; make sure you clean this kitchen." I'm doing it now."

Alvenia cleaned the kitchen then went into her room to pick out something to wear for her senior pictures. Sunday a week later, Jessica trimmed and styled her hair. The next day was picture day. Before she got out, Jessica said," Take a nice picture Alvey." When Alvenia went inside, 2 girls made fun of her. First a Puerto Rican girl named Julianna. She said, "Look at raggedy Ann, she's fixed up today; I wonder where she got that dress, it looks like one of Good-Will's best." (they laugh) The other girl was white. Her name was Daphne. "Her hair looks pretty, but my grandmother used to wear the same shoes to work." (They laughed and continued their jokes). Then a black girl who stood 5'9, and weighed 135 pounds stepped up. Her name was Colleen. She was a beautiful girl with flawless dark skin, and had a humongous afro. "Leave her alone! You have nothing else better to do but harass someone?!" "Well excuse us!" "Yeah excuse you! Scram! Go find a dog bone to gnaw on!"

"Thank you, Colleen." Alvenia said, looking scared. "No problem, and don't pay them any attention, Alvenia: You look pretty." "Thank you." "You don't have to thank me. By the way, Alvenia' can I call you at your home?" "I have a phone but it'll be best if I call you." "Okay, here's my number: Call me when you get a chance." "I will, and we better get to class." Yeah, take a nice picture, Alvenia." "I'll try, and You too, Colleen."

That evening Jessica took Alvenia home then went to the beauty salon. Alvenia watched her leave then hurried out back to go see, Francine. She knocked. "Yes!" "It's Alvenia, Miss Francine." "Come in Dear!" Alvenia went in. "You look pretty; sit down." Said Francine, smiling. "Thank you." "Where have you been?" "I took my senior pictures today." "You've trimmed your hair: It's pretty." Alvenia chuckled. "Aunt Jessie did it." "Did she?" "Yes, ma'am." "I like it." Alvenia smiled as Francine stared at her. "Alvenia, what's your shoe size?" "6 and a half and some 7's." "I'm wearing a 7: Come with me to my closet." Said Francine.

She had a walk-in closet 10'12" wide. She asked Alvenia to open the doors. She opened them and said, "WOW! You have so many shoes: They're very pretty, too." "Take a few." Said Francine. "You mean I can take whatever I want?" "Yes, anything but the 3 pair sitting there in the front, and the 3 at the bottom of that rack." Alvenia got excited and grabbed 5 pairs. "Did you get all you want?" Francine asked, very giving. "Yes maám. "Are you sure?" "Yes, these are more than enough. You have very good taste, ma'am." "Thanks, Dear." "You're welcome and thank you for these shoes, ma'am." "No problem, Sweetie; anything I can do for you, I will. So, don't hesitate to ask. Alright?" "Alright, ma'am." As Alvenia gathered the shoes, she suddenly said, "Wait." "What is it, Dear?" Francine asked, very concerned. Alvenia said, "I can't take these shoes home." "Why not?" "My aunt will ask me where I got them. Then she'll say I begged you and shouldn't have come here." "I'll tell you what, leave them here; I'll see that you get them without her knowing." "Okay, ma'am. And ma'am, please don't let Miss Betty know I was here." "No worries, this will be another one of our secrets." "I'm going to leave now: I have to cook dinner." "Alright, Sweetie."

The next day at 5:15 p.m., Alvenia was in the den doing some homework. Jessica went in there. "I'm going out with Betty Lou for a while." "When?" Alvenia asked. "Around 7: Don't wait up for me tonight." At 6:45 p.m., Alvenia was still in the den. Jessica went back in there. She was carrying a large tote bag. "I'm leaving, Alvey! Here." "What's that?" "Some shoes, Betty Lou gave you; Her aunt was sending them to Good-Will, but she thought about you. Here, I have to go: Betty Lou's out there waiting for me." "Tell them I said thanks." "I will and don't forget to close up the house. And please don't open the door for anyone, Alvey." "I won't. Have fun!" Jessica thought, "she never told me to have fun: It must be the shoes, I hope she likes them."

Alvenia grabbed the bag from the other end of the sofa. She smiled after she opened it. Then said, "Miss Francine is very smart; She gave me all of them and this extra pair. They're beautiful, and new, too. If it wasn't dark, I'll go over and thank her." Francine had someone to buy that extra pair of shoes and bring them to her. It was one of her secrets from Betty Lou.

The next day, Alvenia wore the extra pair of shoes to school. They were so beautiful, the girls made fun of her were jealous. Later that evening she called Colleen. "Hi, Colleen." "Who's this?" Colleen asked. "It's, Alvenia Hutchinson." "Hi, Alvenia." "What are you doing, Colleen?" "I'm watching tv." "What are you watching?" "Bonanza." "I watch Bonanza, too: I like all Westerners." "Yeah me too: The Big Valley: Gunsmoke: Rifleman: The Virginian; all of them." Said Colleen.

Alvenia went on and said," I called to thank you again, Colleen." "For what?" "Taking up for me the other day." "Oh, that's no problem; those girls have nothing else to do. I believe they go to school just to harass someone; They're definitely not doing anything in class. By the way Alvenia, I like those cut out heels you were wearing today. Do you know every girl wishes they had a pair?" "No, I didn't know that." "Well they do; Their very popular shoes, Alvenia. Who bought them for you?" "One of my aunt's friends." "They sure do have good taste. I've seen people like, 'Cher Bono', 'Diana Ross', and that Model, 'Iman', wearing those shoes." "I like them, too, but I didn't know they were that popular." Said Alvenia, with a smile. Colleen added, "That's real (Cherokee leather), girl. Alvenia then whispered," I have to go, Colleen. I'll talk to you later." "I'll be right there, Aunt Jessie!" Alvenia went to Jessica's room. "Yes, Aunt Jessie?" "Run my bath; and have you finished your homework?" "Yes, ma'am." "From now on do it before dark because the electrical bill has gone up." "Okay, your bath is ready; anything else?" "Yeah, the other day I called the phone was busy. Who were you talking too; I hope it wasn't a boy." "It wasn't. It was a girl from my school." "Who is she?" Jessica asked. "Her name is 'Colleen Dixon'." "Is she a black girl?" "Yes, she is." "That might be the Colleen who Betty Lou mentioned a couple of times. I don't know, maybe. But anyway, what do you and Colleen talk about that you can't at school?" "Nothing, Aunt Jessie." "We'll talk about nothing at school!" "Yes, ma'am." "You can go now." Said Jessica.

CHAPTER 3

What a Friend

A FEW DAYS passed. Jessica and Betty Lou had plans for that Sunday. Alvenia couldn't wait for them to leave. So, she kept busy until Jessica was ready at 5:30 pm. "I'm leaving Alvey; I'll probably be out for a few hours. I'm going to call you, so don't tie up the phone. See you later!" "Okay." Said Alvenia. Then she waited a few minutes before she put on her sneakers and hurried over to see her friend, Francine. After she'd reached the edge of her yard, she noticed Jessica's car in the drive-way. She was there half an hour before her and Betty Lou finally left. "It's about time; I thought they'd never leave." Alvenia said, rushing to Francine's door.

She knocked, but didn't get an answer. She knocked again, and still no answer. "I know she's there." As Alvenia began to walk away she heard a noise. That time she tapped on the window. "Miss Francine are you in there?!" "Yes!" "Are you okay, ma'am?!" "Yes, Dear; come back another day!" "Alright, ma'am!" Alvenia left with a crushed spirit. She went home and watched a movie, then went to bed early. At 6: a.m., she got up to use the bathroom. While there she heard Jessica talking to someone. She thought, 'Who's she talking too?' Afterwards, she left the bathroom and creeped down the hall to listen. She heard a man's voice. He said," You know I've always wanted you, Jessica." Jessica said, "Maybe you have, but you know I'm raising my niece: Let's see what happens after she finishes school." The man said," She seems like a nice kid; and besides that, she's almost grown." "I know but she's been in my way all these years. I never wanted any kids; I had no other choice but to take her. My mother had diabetes so bad she had to go into a nursing home; She's still there, and so is my father. Things haven't been easy for me." "I better be going Jessica." "I know Pete, you have to get back to your wife; what a friend." Alvenia creeped back to her room.

At 7:30 a.m., Jessica bangs on her door. "Open this door Alvey!" Alvenia got out of bed and faked a yawn as she opened the door. "Why were you out of bed at 6 o'clock?" Jessica asked. "I went to the bathroom." "Well just to let you know, you can't creep on these wood floors; They're too old. Hurry up. I'm off today but I have a few things to do." Alvenia mumbled: "I bet you do, and going to see Mr. Pete is probably one."

As she got out at school, Jessica said, "I might be a few minutes late this evening." "Are you going to buy groceries?" "Maybe." "Get some apples, please." "I'll think about it." "Bye!" Said Alvenia, while closing the car door. When she went inside, Colleen was standing by the front entrance. "Hi, Colleen." "Hi, I was waiting for you Alvenia." "Why?" "Are you going on the field trip?" "Which one?" "Van Cortlandt Park." "I forgot about that; I'll have to check and see." "You better hurry; the deadline is in a couple of days."

"Thanks for telling me. By the way, how do you get to school, Colleen?" "I drive." "You drive?" Alvenia asked, surprised. Colleen said," Yeah, my mom works at night and I have to take my little sister and brother to school. So, my grandmother lets me use her car." "How long have you been driving?" "A couple of years, but I've had my driver's license only a year." "That's great." "Yeah, it is and we better get to our class." Said Colleen. Later that day, Alvenia saw her driving away in her grandmother's brown '1969 Buick Riviera'.

That evening she called her. "Hi, Alvenia; what's up?" "I saw you leaving today: I like your grandmother's car." Colleen laughed and said," It's big isn't it?" "Yeah, but it's a nice car. I wish I knew how to drive: when did you learn, Colleen?" "My father taught me when I was 14." "Are you allowed to take the car whenever you want?" "I normally use it to take my sister and brother to school, and yes I go by myself sometimes." "I hope I'm not asking too many questions." "No; ask me anything you want, Alvenia." "Alright, how far have you driven?" "I'll put it this way, I've never left The Bronx." "Well at least you're driving." "Yes, and I don't mean to cut our conversation Alvenia, but I have to go now; I'll see you tomorrow at school." "Bye."

Jessica was in the den watching tv. "Alvey!" She yelled. "Yes!" "Bring me a glass of water!" After Alvenia gave her the water, she tempted to ask her a question. But Jessica cut her off. "Not now Alvey, I'm trying to see the end of this movie." That saddened Alvenia. She went back to her room and got in bed. 20 minutes later, Jessica turned off the television, then headed to her room. On the way she stopped at Alvenia's. "Alvey you should know not to bother me when I'm watching a movie: what did you want?" "I forgot." "You interrupt me at the end of a movie and all you can say is you forgot?!" "I'm sorry Aunt Jessie." "Yeah you're sorry! Go back to bed!"

Early the next day, Jessica was still in bed while Alvenia got dressed. Afterwards she went and made coffee and took Jessica a cup. "Here Aunt Jessie." Jessica setup quickly. "Oh my, I was dreaming. What time is it?" She asked. "Almost 7 a.m." "Sometimes I wish you can take yourself to school." "That's it. That's it!" Said Alvenia. "What are you talking about?" "That's what I wanted to ask you." "I'm not going to ask you again Alvey: what are you trying to say?" "Last night I was about to ask if you'll teach me how to drive." "Teach you how to drive?"

"Yes!" Said Alvenia. Jessica laughed. (ha ha ha!) "I thought it was something important. Go on out of here Alvey."

The next morning on the way to Alvenia's school, she said, "I really do want to learn how to drive, Aunt Jessie." "I don't have time to teach you Alvey; and besides, this hoopty is too raggedy: do you want to tear it up more?" "I just thought to ask." "Well it's not happening. Not now anyway." They arrived at the school. Jessica said, "I might be late this evening." Alvenia saw Colleen and began to rush. "Okay Aunt Jessie. Bye!" "Colleen!" "Hey, Alvenia!" "I need to talk to you, Colleen!" "I'm in a hurry, Alvenia! I'll talk to you doing lunch; meet me in the cafeteria!" Said Colleen, shouting. "Okay!"

Alvenia didn't like going to the school's cafeteria, but she went that afternoon. Colleen was sitting at a table near the entrance. There were a couple of Hispanic and African American girls sitting with her. Alvenia went over and sat next to Colleen. Afterwards a few of the girls had a smirk on their face. "Is there a problem?" Colleen asked. One of the girls got up and left. Colleen went on and said, "Do anybody want to follow that fly; if so, help yourself." No one moved. "Hi Alvenia." "Hi Colleen. Are you almost done?" Alvenia asked. "Yeah give me a minute. Better yet, I'll take this orange with me. Let's get out of here. Latrina, Cassandra, Marquita, Tiffany, I'll catch up with you later." Colleen said. "Later girl!" After Colleen said bye to her friends, Alvenia wanted to go to the auditorium. They went and sat in the back. "What do you want to talk to me about, Alvenia?" "I was wondering if you could teach me how to drive?" "Have you ever considered taking Driver's Ed?" (Driver's Education) "Yes, but I'm not allowed to take any evening classes." "I don't know Alvenia, I normally don't use the car on weekends." Said Colleen, seriously. "Well I just thought to ask." "You seem to be anxious: is there a reason why?" "I want to learn before I graduate." "Have you asked your aunt?" Alvenia exhaled before saying: "Yeah I asked. She said our car is in too bad of shape." "I'm sorry I can't help you." "It's okay, Colleen." "Maybe something will work out for you later, Alvenia." "I hope so." "It will and there's the bell: time to go." As they exit the auditorium, Colleen said," I just thought of something Alvenia, but we don't have time to talk about it now; call me tonight." "Okay I will." Said Alvenia, walking away.

That evening, Jessica was late. "Where have you been; I've waited almost an hour." I told you this morning I might be late, Alvey." "I forgot and it's hot out here!" "Are you raising your voice at me, Missy?!" Jessica asked. "No ma'am." "Well tone it down! I'm in no mood today!" "Yes, ma'am." "I bought some yams." "Okay." Alvenia wasn't too happy, but she was glad to hear Jessica says she'd bought some yams: They were her backup for use of the cinnamon when she baked cookies for Francine.

When they got home, Jessica went in the den and flopped on the sofa. Alvenia went to her room and did her homework. An hour later, she went to the den. "Aunt Jessie, I need some (pads)." "Why didn't you tell me earlier, Alvey?" "I wasn't expecting it today." "Give me my purse; I'll be back.

Alvenia made up the story about the pads, to get Jessica out of the house. She was desperate to call Colleen. "Hello, may I speak to Colleen?" "Hold on." "It's for you, Colleen." Said Colleen's little sister. Colleen, took the phone from her. "Hello." "It's Alvenia, Colleen. I can't talk but a few minutes." "Alright, here's what I thought, Alvenia: If you could write your aunts signature and give the school a letter to be let out early 3 days next week, I'll get out early, too; that way I can teach you how to drive." "Really?" "Yeah, but you'll have to learn in those 3 days, because we don't want to do that again." "So, I have to write a letter and sign my aunt's signature?" Alvenia asked. "I'll write the letter. You just make sure you have your aunt's signature down packed." "I don't follow you; what's down packed?" Colleen laughed. "Just colloquialism of making that signature perfect." "Okay, I got it." Alvenia said. "Alright then. I'll bring the letter tomorrow." "Thanks, Colleen. Bye."

Jessica walked in with the pads. "Here Alvey." "Thank you." Alvenia said. "Listen Alvey' I forgot I have a meeting at the hospital. I'll be back around 8:00 p.m.; go ahead and make dinner, and cook the yams the way you did the last time." "Is Miss Betty going to the meeting?" "Yes, I'm riding with her; we're leaving now." After Jessica walked out, Alvenia went to her room to find something with her signature. It didn't take long, she found it in one of her books. Afterwards, she hid the book under her bed mattress and thought," I'll get to it later; I'm going to see, Miss Francine."

Alvenia cooked white rice, field peas, candy yams, fried chicken, and baked 12 cinnamon cookies in 1 hour. As that's how eager she was to see Francine. She put the chicken in the oven to keep warm, and the cookies in a Ziploc bag. At 6:15 pm, she was on her way. She'd always peek through Francine's window before she knocked. She was lying down. "That's gotta be Alvenia; She's the only person who knocks on the door. "Yes!" "It's, Alvenia ma'am!" "Hold on a minute!" Francine said, as she turned on the tv and went and opened the door. "Hello Alvenia. Come in and have a seat: I'll sit back down here." "Take your time, ma'am." "How have you been?" Francine asked. "I've been okay." "Just ok?" "Yes ma'am: Nothing really to complain about." "That's something to be grateful for, Dear."

"Here ma'am. I bought you some cookies." "Thank you. They smell so good." "Ma'am, you have a bruise on your face; what happened?" "The other day I was reaching for my walker and fell." "It looks awful." Said Alvenia, concerned. "I'm okay, Sweetie." "Are you sure, ma'am?" "Yes, and enough about me. How has school been?" 'It's been okay: I'm graduating this summer." "That's good." "It would be better if I could go to college." "Why can't you?" "I was accepted by 3 schools, but Aunt Jessie said I have to wait a while." "She told you that?" "Yes, and Please don't say anything to Miss Betty." "What's the name of those schools?" "(UCLA) University of California, John C. Hopkins, and (UM) University of Miami." "Those are good schools; maybe things will change." "I don't think so; I really believe my aunt wants me to keep cooking and cleaning up after her."

Francine took a cookie from the bag and bit it. "These cookies are delicious. I'd say you're getting better and better." Alvenia smiled and said," It's getting dark, I better go." "Yes, and don't wait long to come see me again." Alvenia bent and hugged Francine. "Miss Francine, is it ok if I called you, Mama Fran?" She asked. Francine let go, then looked up at Alvenia. Her left eye was almost shut. "Under one condition." Alvenia asked, "What, ma'am?" "If you let me call you, Cookie." That stunned, Alvenia. She embraced Francine tighter. Francine felt her love. Her eyes watered. "Yes, I would love that, ma'am." "Alright, go on now Sweetie." "Don't get up ma'am; I'll lock the door. And I'll try to come back tomorrow. Bye!" "I love that girl. She's so sweet."

"Who are you talking to, Aunt Fran?" Betty Lou asked. "I was just laughing at a commercial: How long have you been back?" "5 minutes: I had to use the bathroom." "I thought you'd be gone a while." "They postponed the meeting." "Where's Jessica?" Francine asked, thinking about Alvenia.

"She's at home. Do you need anything, Aunt Fran?" "No." "Alright, I'm going to lie down." Francine thought, 'I hope Alvenia is ok.' Alvenia heard Jessica's car engine just before she entered her yard. As that's how loud it was. "Why is she back so soon? I better hurry." As she entered the back door, Jessica was walking in the front. "Is that you, Aunt Jessie?!" "Yes, I'm back and ready to eat; bring my food to my room!" "Okay!" Alvenia said, loudly. Her adrenaline sword at the thought of Jessica finding out she'd left. She gave her dinner, then went and practiced writing her signature. She practiced for a couple of hours. Then just as she was putting the book away, Jessica knocked. "Alvey!" "Just a minute." "Why is the door locked?" "I'm changing my pad." But there's no one here but us." "I know. Give me a minute." "That's okay; it's nothing important." Said Jessica.

The next morning during breakfast, Jessica said, "You should change your pads in the bathroom; We don't have money to clean blood stains off the carpet." "I'm always careful." "Things happen, Alvey! I'll be glad when you finish school, too: it'll be much of a pleasure taking you to work every day." "Why did you say that, Aunt Jessie?" "Because the money I get for you is about to stop, and I'm sure the money you earn will be much more." "I still wish I could go to college." I don't wanna talk about that! I told you you'll go later! Are you done eating?!" "Yes." Alvenia said, feeling dejected. "Let's go then." Jessica said, feeling no pity.

After Alvenia was dropped off, Colleen was there waiting. "Hey Colleen." "Hi. Have you been practicing?" "Yeah." "Well here's the letter; It's dated for Wednesday." Thanks. I'm going to practice some more this weekend." "Good." "I'm ready!" Alvenia said. (Colleen laughed, Alvenia smiled) Then Alvenia suddenly said, "Oh and Colleen' I'm going to eat lunch in the cafeteria today." "Are you sure?" "Yes." "Where do you normally go, Alvenia?" "I stay in my English class." "Miss Medley let you stay in there?" "Yeah." 'That's good; You don't have to be bothered by anyone." "I know and that's how I like it." (they laughed again) Alvenia, submitted the early release letter the next day, and everything went accordingly. Then after a few days, she thanked Colleen for teaching her how to drive. She was so excited that Jessica noticed a change in her behavior.

On their way home that Friday evening she said," You seemed to be happy about something." I do? "Yeah, what is it?" "I guess I'm glad my period went off." "But you've never seemed that happy." "I've never cramped the way I did either: They were really bad." "Yeah, they can be uncomfortable. When we get home, I'm going to watch a movie. There's a good one coming on; why don't you watch it with me, Alvey?" "I can't, I have makeup work, Aunt Jessie." "Why do you have makeup work?" "Is that what I said?" "Yeah." "Well I meant homework."

When they got home, Alvenia went to her room and exhaled. She was hoping Jessica didn't find out she'd learned how to drive, and couldn't wait to share her good news with Francine.

Saturday afternoon, Jessica and Betty Lou went to their meeting at the hospital. They told Francine and Alvenia it'll be over at 4pm. That made Alvenia happy. She did some dusting, watered a few plants, then went to see Francine. After she'd arrived, she peeked through the window and saw Francine walking from the bathroom. She knocked. "Is that you, Cookie?!" "Yes ma'am!" "I'll be right there." Francine went and opened the door. "Hi Cookie, come in and have a seat. How are you?" She said. As Alvenia set down she answered, "I'm good. How are you, ma'am?" "Mama Fran is feeling fine today, Sweetie." "Well good. I noticed the bruise is gone."

"Yes, it is. I'll tell you' sometimes I'm like a child." "What do you mean, ma'am?" "Clumsy." Alvenia giggled. Francine, held up her right hand and said," If I'm not falling, I'm knocking over something." Then she laughed. (ha ha ha!) "Mama Fran, is that a bruise on your risk?" "What? This?"

"Yes." "That must've happened earlier when I was coming in from outside: I wobbled and hit my arm on the door." Alvenia asked, "Does it hurt?" "It's a little sore." Said Francine.

Alvenia stared at Francine's discolored risk, then looked her straight in the eyes and asked, "Did Miss betty do that to you?" Francine answered," No, and why would you ask me that?" "Because it happened to me when I was younger." "What happened to you, Dear?" "Whenever I flustered Aunt Jessie, she'd shove me, or hit me real hard. And when I had bruise marks, she made me wear clothes to hide them." "Are you telling me she's treated you that bad?" "Yes, ma'am. Now it's more verbal. She's always hurting my feelings. That's why I wish I could leave." "Now hold on, Cookie', you're about to graduate and things could change." "No, it's not. She's waiting for me to graduate and start working: It's practically all she talks about."

Francine looked Alvenia in the eyes and said," I'm going to be honest with you, Cookie'. Betty Lou, has been mean to me, and for a very long time. You see, she's an only child, and her father was my husband's brother. After he'd died, my husband and I adopted her. She loved her Uncle Franklin. But she never liked me. And during the time of his passing, she was the only somebody to take care of me. And she never changed. There have been many times I wished I could just pick up and leave, too." "I'm so sorry for you, Mama Fran." "It's okay, Hon; Mama Fran is going to be alright." "Are you sure?" "Yes, I'm sure. If I just had someone to take me out sometimes. It'll make me feel a lot better." "Where would you go?" "To the Park; I'll sit in the shade, breathe fresher air, look at the doves, and watch the birds fly. Or go to the store and buy my things, rather than ordering from magazines."

"Miss Betty never take you out?" "Very seldom. She takes me mostly to the bank to get money for her." "But she works." Said Alvenia. "Yes, she does, and waste every cent of her earnings." "This is her house isn't it?" "It was before I paid for it." "WOW! Miss Betty talks like this is her house." Alvenia said, surprised. "I know, and the car, too." "The car is yours?" "Yes."

"Mama Fran I have something to tell you, and this needs to be one of our secrets." "What is it, Hon?" "Theirs 1 girl at my school that's been nice to me." "What's her name?" "Colleen: She's black." "She has a Pretty name." Said Francine. "Guess what, ma'am?" "I don't know. What?" "She taught me how to drive." "You're joking! When?! How?!" "We put together a note for me to be let out of school early. Then we went out on the back roads. I got the feel of it after a few days. Now I know how to drive." "What a friend." Francine said, happy for Alvenia. "Yes, she is. I was going to tell you about this the day you weren't feeling well, ma'am.

Hold up, when I came back to see you, you had that bruise on your face. Did Miss Betty do that to you?" "Yes, she did." "You told me you fell." "I know and let's not worry about that; We need to focus on how you can get your driver's license. And don't you speak of this to anyone." Said Francine. "Yes ma'am, I won't; especially not to Aunt Jessie." "That's right. I'm going to see what I can do, but I have a question for you, Cookie." "Sure, what is it ma'am." "Do you know if Jessica is going to the hospital's picnic?" "Like the one they had last year at Orchard Beach?" Alvenia asked. "Yes; They say it's their Spring Picnic."

"I'm not sure ma'am, but I believe I heard her talking about it to someone on the telephone." "That picnic's in a couple of weeks; You need to find out if she's going as soon as possible, and let me know, Cookie." "I will, and you be careful, Mama Fran." Don't fret over me, Dear: I'm going to be fine. You better go now. And remember our secret, Cookie." "Yes, ma'am. Bye!"

Alvenia walked out with tears in her eyes after finding out what her dear friend was enduring. On her way home she reminisced about some of her abuse from Jessica. Meanwhile, Francine pondered and said, "It's a shameful disgrace how Jessica's been to that girl. It's a wonder she hasn't left or ran away."

CHAPTER 4

Driving Privileges

ALVENIA WAS GREATLY saddened by her friend; She cried all the way home. She went in, cleaned herself up, and made dinner. When Jessica got home, she did her usual, then went to her room. Minutes later, Alvenia went in there. "Do you want your dinner now, Aunt Jessie?" "No, I'm not hungry." "Okay, I'm going to my room." Said Alvenia. On the way to her room she said," I need to find out if she's going to that picnic: I'll figure out something." "Alvey!" "What does she want now? Yes, Aunt Jessie?!" "Bring me my dinner!" "Okay! I'm really sick of her, I should just ask her if she's going to that picnic."

Moments later, Alvenia took her her dinner. She sat on the edge of the bed, then took the plate. "Did you beat the meat?" She asked. "Yes." Alvenia answered, irritated. Jessica said, "Good; I hate when it's tough. You can go now." "Aunt Jessie'." "What is it?" "Wasn't it this time last year your job had that picnic?" Jessica' spread butter on her bread roll. "You remember that?" She asked. Alvenia replied, "Yes. It was right after I took my school pictures." "It's the hospital's Spring picnic, Alvey; They're doing it in a couple of weeks." "Are you going?" "I plan, too. Can I eat now please?"

Alvenia walked out happy. She said, "Good, she's going to the picnic."

The next day on their way to 'August M. High', Jessica said," Last night I told you my job's picnic was in a couple of weeks, I forgot they moved it up: It's this weekend." "Is Miss Betty going?" "Sure, that's my ride." "What time does it start?" Alvenia asked. "It's from 1 to 5, but I doubt if we stay that long: We'll probably leave around 4." "That's plenty of time to enjoy yourself." "Yeah, it is. I'll see you later." Said Jessica.

That afternoon, Alvenia was asked to go to the office. She was shocked after she walked in and saw Jessica talking to the attendance clerk. She heard the clerk say:" She was just released early." Then she interrupted and said," Aunt Jessie, what are you doing here?" "I come to get you." "Why?" Alvenia asked. Jessica said, "I was out and suddenly got sick: I'm going home and lying down and not coming back out." The clerk begins to speak, Alvenia interrupted again. "Didn't you hear my aunt say she wasn't feeling well?" "Alright, I hope to see you tomorrow Alvenia." "Let's go Aunt Jessie."

When they got in the car, Jessica put her head on the steering wheel. "Are you okay Aunt Jessie?" "Yeah, just give me a minute." After a moment, Jessica held her head up. "I like the way you spoke up for me to that lady, but don't ever do that again: I can speak for myself, Alvey." "Yes ma'am." Alvenia was glad she walked in on time to interrupt the clerk from telling Jessica she'd been released early 3 times that month.

After they'd made it home, Jessica got in bed and stayed there for the rest of the evening. The next morning, Alvenia took her breakfast. "How are you feeling?" She asked. "I feel fine Alvey: It must've been a bug." "I thought your picnic was in a couple of days." "Yes, it is. Which reminds me that me and Betty Lou are going to the mall today; I might be late this evening."

"It's okay, I'll wait." "You have no other choice." "I know, Aunt Jessie." Said Alvenia, being calm as usual.

When school let out, Jessica was there. "Hey, I thought you were going to the mall." "I was but Betty Lou had to take her aunt somewhere: We're going after I take you home." When they got home, Betty Lou was already there. "Ha, ha, ha, she's already here. Hey Girl! Give me a minute!" Said Jessica. She went and opened the door for Alvenia. "You don't have to cook dinner Alvey; I'm eating out." Alvenia said," Okay then went inside and locked the door. After a moment, she shouted, "Yes!" As That's how happy she was to see Jessica leave.

20 minutes later, Francine here's a knock. "Yes?!" "It's Alvenia!" "Hold on Dear, I'm coming! "Come in." "How are you, Mama Fran?" "Pretty fare. How about yourself?" "I have some good news." Alvenia said, smiling.

"What is it, Cookie?" "Aunt Jessie is going to that picnic." "That's wonderful news." Francine said, smiling, too. "But it's this Saturday, ma'am." Francine got very comfortable and said," That's alright, Hon. Here's what I thought, the (DMV) is open on Saturday." "What's the (DMV)?" "Drivers of Motor Vehicles." "So that's the place where you get your driver's license?" "Yes, and they're open from 9:30 pm to 3:30 pm." "But ma'am, I don't know how I'm going to get there." "Hold on and listen to me Cookie, I was thinking maybe your friend can take you." "I don't know about that ma'am. Even if she could, I don't have any money to pay her." Don't worry about money, I have to give tW you." "Ma'am I don't want to take your money." "You're not taking, I'm giving it. Just hope your friend can take you. That would be great." "You're right, but I can't leave until after Aunt Jessie leaves, and be back before her." "Pray about it: You do know how to pray, don't you?" "Yes ma'am." "That's very good.

Go get that jewelry box from the top draw of my chest and bring it to me." Alvenia got the box and set it on Francine's lap. She opened it and said, "Here's 50 dollars. It's more than enough for the driver's exam, and you can give your friend something for taking you. If she doesn't charge you, offer her something anyway. And make sure you have a good place to put up what's left." "I will ma'am, thank you."

Where's Jessica?" "She and Miss Betty went shopping." "That's right. I forgot they went shopping." "You knew they went shopping?" "Yes, Betty Lou took me to the bank this afternoon. But little did she know, I let her have that time to get that money for you, Cookie." Alvenia laughed: (ha ha)! "Ma'am I have to water some plants, so I'm going to leave now: don't get up, I'll lock the door." "Alright, Sweetie. And make sure you get a good night's rest, and when you take the test, relax and concentrate; Then maybe you'll have your license when I see you again." "I hope so, ma'am." "I'm going to (pray) for you, Sweetie." "Okay, Bye!" "Bye!"

Alvenia went home and called Colleen. "Hello Colleen." "Hey Alvenia! Is everything good?!" "Yes, but I have a question for you." "Okay, what is it?" "If it's not a problem on Saturday, can you take me to do the driver's license exam?" "This Saturday?" Colleen asked. "Yes." "Well it depends on the time; I have to take my grandmother to do her grocery shopping." "They're open until 3:30. So I was thinking maybe at 2:00." Alvenia said. "I'll let you know tomorrow, Alvenia." "Thanks Colleen."

Alvenia hung up with Colleen, then went outside to water some plants. On her way back in, Jessica and Betty Lou drove up. "Hi Alvey!" Betty Lou said. Alvenia waved. "Hi Miss Betty!" Betty Lou turned to Jessica and said," Alvey is becoming a beautiful young lady, Jessica." "I know, and hope it doesn't go to her head: that's why I don't let her wear the fancy stuff." "I hear you, and I guess I'll go see what my tired aunt is up too." "She's a sweet lady, Betty Lou." "Yeah, when she wants to be." "Why do you say that?" Jessica asked. "She's getting tight with her money." 'But you work and she's basically taking care of you: I wish I had it like that." "You said that like I don't take care of her, Jessica." "You feed and bathe her, but you (lack) a lot, Betty Lou." "I can't sit with her all day, Jessica; I have a life." "I feel you on that. But I've been thinking about spending more time with Alvey: She's about to graduate, and I need her dollars to keep coming in."

'Betty Lou' laughed and said," I'll give you a high 5 on that: Got to keep them dollars rolling in." "Yep. Alright Betty Lou, I'll see you later."

"I'm in, Alvey!" "I'm in my room, Aunt jessie!" Jessica went to Alvenia's room. "Hey, did I get any calls?" She asked, standing in the door-way. "No." "Did you water the plants; the Pansies and Begonias really needed it." "I know, I watered all of them." "Good. I'm going to relax a little."

Alvenia went to use the bathroom, thereafter she went to Jessica's room. She was lying across her bed reading a book. Aunt Jessie'? Jessica kept reading. Then after a moment she said," What, Alvey?" "My senior prom is coming up and I want to go." "I don't think that's a good idea." "Why not?" Alvenia asked. Jessica put the book down, then looked up and said," For number one, you don't have the clothes to wear, and who are you going with?" "I don't have to go with anybody." "It just won't be right, Alvey: those kids are going to be well groomed and riding in fancy cars." "Can't you squeeze out a little of the money you get for me?" "No! You don't have any money! It's mind! How do you think you have a place to live, food in your stomach, and a ride to school every day?! Me! I make sure you have all those things! Don't ever say that again to me! Your money! Go on and leave me alone, Alvey!"

Broken-hearted Alvenia went to her room and cried. The next morning on her way to school, Jessica said," I shouldn't have yelled at you last night, but you've got to understand we don't have much." "I missed my 8th grade prom, and I really wanted to go to the senior; It's part of my growing, Aunt Jessie." Alvenia said, emotionally. "Don't worry, later in your life you'll have a lot more to do." "But this is my life now." "I'll tell you what, maybe I'll take you with me to the picnic." "What?" Alvenia asked. Jessica said," My job picnic: do you want to go?" "I'll think about it." "What is there to think about?" "I really don't want to be in your way." How can you be in my way Alvey, it's a picnic; people eating, socializing, and having fun. Probably more than that prom." "Alright, I'll go." "Okay, I'll let Betty Lou know."

They drove up to the school. "See you later!" Said Jessica. When she drove away, Alvenia hit her forehead with the palm of her hand. "Uhhhh, what was I thinking!" she said. That afternoon she saw Colleen in the hall- ways. "Hi Colleen." "Hey Alvenia, are you ready for tomorrow?" "What?" "Are you ready to go to the (DMV) tomorrow?" Colleen asked, smiling. "You're going to take me?" "Yes, I'm sorry I didn't call and tell you." "It's okay, Colleen. Will 2 o'clock be fine?" "Sure, we don't have any plans for tomorrow. I have to go to the office, Alvenia; I'll talk to you later." Colleen said, while walking away. Alvenia pondered. "Now I have to figure out a way to keep from going to that picnic." She said. Then during 4th Period, (Science) a thought occurred. "I'll pretend to be sick, because I'm going to the 'DMV', and besides, she's never asked me to go on a picnic with her; why now?"

That evening during dinner she said," Oh my stomach." "What's wrong?" Jessica asked. "I don't know, I Probably ate too much." "I doubt it. It's probably the cabbage. Leftover cabbage bothers my stomach." "It does?" Alvenia asked, acting ill. Jessica answered, "Yeah, but you'll be fine." "Okay, I'm going to lie down." Said Alvenia. "Go ahead. I'm going to make some calls, then I need to look for something to wear tomorrow. What are you wearing Alvey?" Alvenia rubbed her stomach and answered, "I don't know; maybe my yellow sun-dress." "You should wear your blue jeans with your favorite blouse." "Okayy, I don't want to miss my tv shows." "What shows?" Jessica asked. "Happy Days, Good Times, and Charlie's Angels." "I love Charlie's Angels; It's a good show. I hope you can enjoy them with that upset stomach." Alvenia said," Me, too." Then she went into her room and turned on the television. Afterwards she thought, "You keep thinking I'm watching tv while I finish studying for the driver's exam."

Alvenia studied a while that night, and some the next morning. Later, Jessica knocked. "It's 10:00, Alvey; are you Awake?!" "Yes." Jessica went in. "How are you feeling?" She asked. "My stomach is still a little upset." "I don't think you should go to the picnic." "Me either, Aunt Jessie: I'll go another time." "Alright, Betty Lou is picking me up at 1:00. I'll be back as soon as I could to check on you." "You don't have to do that." "I know I don't." Jessica replied. "I'm just saying I'll be okay, Aunt Jessie." "I should be back around 4." Jessica said.

Betty Lou was prompt, so was Colleen. She and Alvenia arrived at the (DMV) at 2:15 pm. There were 3 people in line ahead of Alvenia. After she was called and did the written exam, she passed it. Then she went back to the waiting area and talked with Colleen. They talked for 20 minutes. Then a driver's examiner asks her to go outside to do the road test: Colleen went with her. After all the road tasks, Alvenia passed everything except the parallel parking. However, the examiner gave her a 2nd chance. "Relax and concentrate, Alvenia." Said Colleen. Alvenia remembered those were the same words, Francine said to her. Then she relaxed, concentrated, and made a perfect park. "The examiner said," Ma'am, drive back to the front and go inside to get your license." Alvenia and Colleen were so excited. They embraced and thanked the examiner.

Then suddenly, Alvenia said," Wait; what time is it?" Colleen looked at her watch. She said, "It's 2:45 pm; what's wrong, Alvenia?" "I've got to go and we need to hurry." "Why hurry?" "You don't know my aunt, Colleen." "But you have to go back inside to get your license." "I know, let's go!" Said

Alvenia. Then after waiting 10 minutes before she was given her license, they were on their way. "I'm very proud of you Alvenia, and your aunt should be, too." "She will, I'm just ready to get home: It looks like it's going to rain and I have a lot to do." But it's Saturday; You should be celebrating." Said Colleen. "I am. I mean I will. Here's ten dollars for taking me." "5 dollar's enough." "Are you sure?" "Yes, I'm sure." "Well thanks for taking me." "No problem, Alvenia. Whenever you need me, I'll help if I can."

Alvenia got home at 3:20. She called Francine at 3:25. Her voice cracked when she answered," Hello?" "Mama Fran it's Alvenia." 'Alvenia'? "Yes ma'am, it's me." "I don't remember giving you this number, Hon." "You didn't, I watched Aunt Jessie dial Miss Betty." "Good for you. How are you doing?" "I got my driver's license ma'am." "Have mercy! I knew you could do it!" "Thank you for everything, Mama Fran." "You don't have to thank me, Cookie; I'm so proud of you." "Okay, I better get off the phone before Aunt Jessie gets here." "Yes, and come see me when you get a chance." "I will. Bye."

Jessica, got home at 4:30. She went to Alvenia's room. "How are you feeling, Alvey?" She asked. "I ate some soup and it made me feel better." Alvenia said, still pretending to be sick. "Jessica went on and said, "You didn't miss anything; we got rained out." Alvenia said, "It didn't rain here, but it was cloudy." "Well, Betty Lou and I went to a bar and had a couple of drinks, and we're going out later. I think you should stay in bed the rest of the evening, Alvey." "That's what I'm doing." "Good, I'm going to my room and relax some myself."

Jessica was off the entire weekend. After hanging out with Betty Lou', she slept all day Sunday. She made Alvenia do her laundry and wash the car, but nothing she did upset Alvenia. As that's how happy she was about having her driver's license. After she'd finished the car, she said," I should go for a quick ride. But I'll wait: I have plenty of time for that."

The next day was 'Memorial Day' Monday. Jessica had to work. Alvenia was glad to be home. She watched tv a while, then went to see Francine. She was surprised to see her sitting on her porch. "Hi, Mama Fran." "Hello my Dear; sit down here next to me." Alvenia set in a lawn chair. "So, you got your driver's license?" "Yes ma'am." "That's really wonderful." "Did you ever drive, Mama Fran?" "Yes, I learned a long time ago. It was 1935, and I'll never forget the day I got my driver's permit. That's what they called it back then. My parents bought me my first car a few weeks later. It was a dark blue (1928 Chrysler). I was so happy' I gave it a name." "Did you?" "Yes. I named it 'Baby'." "Why Baby'?" "Because it took me wherever I needed to go. My mother and father used to ask me where I was going and I'd say," I'm going for a ride with my Baby'. Or, Baby' is taking me to town, and Baby's taking me to the movies. (ha ha ha)! They'd laugh at me." "What happened to Baby?" Alvenia asked. "She got old, and Poppa sold her. I really missed that car. But not long after, I got a part time job and bought myself another one.

I'm just ranting; would you like something to drink, Sweetie?" "Thanks, ma'am; but I'm fine." "Alvenia, have you thought about what you want to do after you graduate?" "Ma'am I really wish I could just leave and go somewhere else." "At times I feel the same way." Said Francine. "Do you?" "Yes, and I believe I will someday." "I really want to go to college, Mama Fran, but my aunt is still against it. Let alone not knowing if

I'm going to be treated badly; They treat me really bad here." "Listen to me, Sweetie, from now on, don't let anybody make you feel inferior. You're smart, you're beautiful, and you can be whatever you want to be." Alvenia grabbed her shirt collar and wiped tears from her eyes. "Don't you cry. Keep those tears out of your eyes and smile as bright as the sun. Do you hear me?" Francine said, while holding Alvenia's chin up with both her hands. "Yes, ma'am I hear you." "Alright Dear, I know you have school tomorrow; come see me again when you can. By the way, do you still have some of that money I gave you?" "Yes." "Good. Try to hold on to it." "Okay ma'am. I'm going to leave now before you know who gets home." "Yes, I know: give me a hug." Francine said, reaching to hug Alvenia tight. After they'd hugged, she said," Don't you worry about nothing; everything's going to be alright. Run along now." "Bye." "Bye, Sweetie." After Alvenia walked away, Francine said, "I guess I better go inside before my none caring niece gets here."

CHAPTER 5

The Good The Bad The Money

MINUTES AFTER FRANCINE was back inside, Betty Lou walked in. "Hey, Aunt Fran." "Heyy." Francine said, while watching tv. "You hungry?" Betty Lou asked. Yes, I'm hungry: You've been gone all day." "You want some fish?" "I'll eat some fish; are you cooking some?" "No. Give me a few dollars; I'll go get some from Big J's." "Jack sale fish?" Francine asked. "Yes, he does." "How come you're just now telling me?" "I don't know, Aunt Fran." Francine took some money from her night stand. She gave it to Betty Lou. "Here's 20 dollars; It should be enough." "Yeah, it's more than enough." "Well bring me some potato wedges, too." "Okay, and I have something to talk to you about when I get back, Aunt Fran." "About what?" "Wait until I get back, lady." Francine' thought, "I hope it's not about money; I'm not giving it to her."

In the meantime, Jessica and Alvenia were having their dinner. "My graduation is in a few weeks, Aunt Jessie." "What's the date?" "June 4th, and school ends on the nineteenth." "That means we need to start looking for you a job." I was looking forward to the Summer break, Aunt Jessie." "You don't need a break; You get one every weekend. I might be able to get you on at the hospital. If that doesn't work, we'll go to some department stores: there's a Wal-Mart not far from us." "I don't want to work at a department store." "You're going to work somewhere; I'm not paying the bills by myself." "Is that why you don't want me to leave?" Alvenia asked. "It's not that I don't want you to leave, just not now, Alvey. I figured you work for a year. Then we'll check out the community college." Alvenia put her fork down and said, "But I have a scholarship!" "Lower that tone of yours, Missy! And clean this kitchen! I'm going to my room." Alvenia was saddened and became more desperate to leave. She cleaned the kitchen, then went to her room and cried.

Betty Lou, made it back. "What took you so long?" Francine asked. "There were quite a few people there." "I smelled the fish when you walked in: It smells good." "I'm going to make our plates." "Hurry I'm hungry!" Betty Lou returned in 5 minutes. She gave Francine her food and set down. Then as Francine took a bite of fish, Betty Lou said, "I have something to tell you, Aunt Fran." "Go ahead I'm listening." Betty Lou went on and said," First I want to know if you remember my friend, Walter?" "He sounds familiar." "You don't remember, Walter?" "Are you talking about the Walter who went to prison a few years ago?" "Yeah." "Is he out?" "Not yet; He's getting out at the end of

June." "Oh yeah?" "Yes, and I told him he could stay here until he gets on his feet." "Why did you tell him that? You' don't pay any bills here, and I'm certainly not going to take care of you and him." "I'm not asking you to take care of him, Aunt Fran!" "Why are you yelling, Betty Lou? Didn't this man leave you for another woman just before he left?" I'm not thinking about that: It's old." You should be thinking about it, because right now he's looking for a place to live, then once he's on his feet, he's going to leave you again: He's a sorry joker." "I think you should let me worry about that." I'm not worried! He can't stay here!" Said Francine, speaking as loud as she could. Betty Lou stood up, then pointed her finger at Francine. "She said," If he doesn't have anywhere to go, he's coming here! Now I've said what I had to say!" She said. After she walked away, Francine said, "And I've said what I had to say."

During the next couple of weeks, Betty Lou and Jessica, partied a lot. Then one afternoon, Alvenia got a call from Francine. "Hello Dear; It's Mama Fran." "Mama Fran?" "Yes, it's me." "I didn't know you had our number, ma'am; what a nice surprise." "I didn't, I got it from the phone book." "Good thinking ma'am." "That was nothing, Hon. Anyway, I called because I really need to talk to you about something." "Is everything okay, ma'am?" "Yes, but I still would like to see you." Francine said. "Alright, tomorrow Aunt Jessie is working the evening shift; I'll come over after she leaves."

Alvenia went to see Francine the next day at 4:30. "Hi, come in. I was coming from the bathroom when you knocked. Sit down and give me a minute; I'm looking for my eyeglasses." "They're on your bed, ma'am." "That's right. I was looking at that magazine and put them there before I went to the bathroom." "That's the Travel Magazine: I like Travel." Alvenia said. "I do too, Cookie." Francine put her glasses on, and gave Alvenia the magazine. Afterwards, she sat in her rocker recliner.

"Is everything okay, Mama Fran?" "I hope so." "You hope so ma'am?"

"Listen to me, Cookie." "I'm listening." Said Alvenia. Francine continued and said, "I've been thinking a lot these last few months. You've had your 18th birthday, and now about to graduate high school; have you decided what you really want to do afterwards?" Ma'am I told you, I want to go to college, but I have to wait a year." "Do you wanna wait?" "I guess I have no choice." "Why, because your aunt said so?" "I don't know, ma'am; all I know is that I want to leave." "Listen to me, Dear', after you turn 18 and finish high school, you can go and come on your own free will. I've thought a lot about you, so I've made preparations for us to leave here." "What?" "You heard correctly. But it's up to you if you want to go." "Go where?" Alvenia asked.

"I've made us hotel reservations for a couple of days." "I haven't graduated yet, Mama Fran." "I know, and the reservation isn't effective until after the last day of school." Ma'am you haven't said where you're going." "You mean, where are we going?" Francine said. "Mama Fran!" "Yes?" "Please tell me what your plans are! My curiosity is killing me!" Francine' laughed. (ha ha ha! I've been in need of some tranquility and longed to leave this place for many years now: Not to mention how badly I want to get from around that mean, selfish, simple mind, Betty Lou'." Then Alvenia laughed. (ha ha ha!) "Is she that bad?" "Baby', you do not want to know all there is to know about Miss Betty Lou."

"So where are we going, Mama Fran? "Washington DC'. My husband and I planned to move there just before our car accident; that's one of the reasons. Then when you told me you were accepted at 'John C. Hopkins University', I later found out it was only minutes away. So, you see, that would be a great start for you, Cookie." "Yes, and it all sounds good, ma'am, but you said the hotel is reserved a couple days, only." "I know, and when the time is up, there's a house waiting for us." "A house?!" "Yes." "Are You kidding, Mama Fran?!" "Nope. I have an old friend who lives there; She arranged everything." "What's going to happen to this house; Isn't it yours?" Alvenia asked. "Yes, and we'll talk about it later. Right now, I need to know if you really want to go with me?" "Let me think for a minute. Yes! Yes! I want to get as far away as I could from my aunt!

Alvenia became very emotional. "I'm so sorry Mama Fran, and please don't get me wrong, I love my aunt, but I am so ready to get away from her: I'm ready to leave." "I know and don't cry, it'll be soon. I've reserved a flight for us, too. Then after we arrive in DC, I have a rental car to pick up: You'll have to drive us to the hotel." "But I don't know anything about that place, ma'am." "Don't worry, I'll show you." "Are you sure?" "Baby', Mama Fran can't move like she used to but I still know my way around." Said Francine, looking Alvenia straight in the eyes. "That's good, ma'am." "Well, I'll try my best. Now, if we're going to do this, you mustn't say a word to anyone, Cookie." "I won't and don't worry ma'am, I'll be ready." "Very good." "I'm going to leave now ma'am." "Alright, call me." "I will." "When Alvenia opened the door, Francine said," Why don't you walk through the neighborhood instead of the woods for a change." "Alright ma'am."

Alvenia left, and for once she walked through her neighborhood, and she and Francine stayed in touch. After 2 weeks passed, one evening while Alvenia prepared dinner, the phone rang. She answered in the kitchen. Jessica answered, too. But the other party hung up without saying anything. 5 minutes later, Jessica went to the kitchen. "Alvey?" "Yes?" Said Alvenia, as she opened the oven. Jessica said, "Did you get a call?" "No. Why?" "2 times today someone called and hung up." "It wasn't for me, Aunt Jessie." "Whoever it is I wish they'd stop. Are you done cooking?" "Almost; I'm waiting on the rice." "After it's done bring my dinner to me." "What do you want to drink?" "Some lemonade; and please don't put too much sugar." Alvenia thought, "I can't wait to get away from here." Moments later, she took Jessica her dinner then went back to the kitchen and enjoyed eating alone.

After a while, the phone rang again. Alvenia answered after Jessica. She decided to listen and covered the phone's receiver with a dish towel. Then she heard Jessica say," You're full of promises, Pete. You've been leading me on since my niece was 12. I told you back then I was ready to put her in a foster home, and now she's grown: I'm not going to ask her to leave until you've committed yourself to me." "You don't have to make her do anything, Jessica. Just live your life the way you want. You said it, she's an adult now." Said Pete Montgomery, the town's market owner. "Unless you marry me, I'm not going anywhere with you, Pete." "Why can't we just leave and think about marriage later, Sweetheart?" "I don't think so, and besides, my niece is getting ready to work: She'll still be able to help me." "Is money all you think about, Jessica? I can give you everything." "Yeah, everything but a wedding ring. Bye Pete!"

Alvenia hung up and set back down. Jessica walked in and put her dishes on the counter. Afterwards, Alvenia became nervous, because she didn't know if Jessica knew she'd been eavesdropping. But, Jessica said, "I have to step out for a while: don't wait up for me." "Aunt Jessie?" "What is it now, Alvey; can't you see I'm on my way out?" "Yes, and I just want to know when we're going job searching?" Alvenia asked, reluctantly. "I've already taken care of that." "What do you mean?" "After you said you didn't want to work at a department store, I went and spoke to the supervisor at the Quality Inn Hotel: She told me to bring you soon after school was out." That shocked Alvenia. She said, "Hotel?" Jessica answered. "Yeah, you'll be cleaning rooms; that shouldn't be too hard. "I guess not." Said Alvenia. "You'll be fine. I have to go now." Said Jessica.

Alvenia washed their few dishes then called Francine. She didn't answer. Then on her way to her room, the phone rang. She rushed to answer. "Hello!" "Alvenia?" "Yes?" "Hi, it's Mama Fran." "Hi, I just called you." Said Alvenia. "I heard it on my way inside, and I called you, too." Said Francine. "Mama Fran, did you call and didn't say anything?" Francine giggled then said, "Yes, and Jessica answered. It's near that time; I called to see if you've done everything?" "Yes, I'm ready. And I just heard Aunt Jessie tell somebody she wanted to put me in a foster home." "Really?" "Yes ma'am. But get this,' she said now she wants me to stay here and pay her bills." "Who did she tell that?" "I don't think you know him ma'am." "Him who?" "Mr. Montgomery; He's the owner of Pete's Food Mart." "I know Peter Montgomery." "Do you, ma'am?" "Yes. I used to buy all of his boil peanuts. That was years ago, and he does have a reputation of being a lady's man." "Isn't he married?" "Yes, he's had about 3 wives." "WOW!" Said Alvenia. "I'll tell you, he's something else Hon." "I believe Aunt Jessie is one of his ladies. I think she's out with him right now." "Don't worry about them, concentrate on your graduation, and be prepared to leave. Mama Fran has everything under control; Alright?" "Alright ma'am. I'll talk to you soon. Bye." "Bye Sweetie." Francine said, kindly.

CHAPTER 6

Work or School

AS GRADUATION APPROACHED, Alvenia was getting excited. But she had to be very careful not to let Jessica find out about her plans. That Tuesday evening, she said, "Graduation rehearsal starts tomorrow, Aunt Jessie." "So, graduation is next Tuesday; Right?" "Yes, and Friday is the last day of school." "That's great; You'll finally be done with school, and can start work Monday." "Yeah, I can. You're coming to my graduation, aren't you?" "I'll try to make it, Alvey: what time does it start?" "11:30." "That means I'll have to take that day off. I guess I'll be there." "One other thing, Aunt Jessie, I need a new dress and shoes." "I don't know about that, Alvey." "Think about it, please!" "Alright, maybe. See you later, and don't slam that door!" "I'm not." Said Alvenia.

That whole afternoon, Alvenia wondered how she and Francine were leaving without, Jessica and Betty Lou finding out. After school let out, Jessica was there waiting. "Hey, how long have you been here?" Alvenia asked. "About 20 minutes; I got off early and took care of some business."

When they got home, Jessica went to her room. Alvenia put away her back pack, then went and made dinner. As she placed chicken in a skillet of hot cooking oil, Jessica walked in with a couple of dresses. "You can look at these, Alvey; I'm going to put them on your bed." "Okay, I'll look at them after dinner."

During dinner, Jessica said, "Those dresses are a little big for you, but with the gown on no one will notice, and you can wear a pair of the shoes Betty Lou gave, too." "I wish I could wear something new: It's my graduation." Alvenia said, looking down at her food. "I've told you several times that we don't have money to shop for a lot, Alvey." "You wear new stuff, why can't I?" "I work, Missy'; I'm going to buy new things for myself! When you work' you'll get new things, too!" "But you get money for me, Aunt Jessie!" Alvenia exclaimed. "I told you that's my money! Clean this kitchen; I'm going to my room to watch the news! Said Jessica. Alvenia left the kitchen, then tried on the dresses. They were too big. She thought, "I'll wear one of my own with my favorite shoes." Afterwards, she went in the den and watched a movie.

The next day at school, she saw Colleen'. "Hey Alvenia, are you ready for graduation?" "Yeah." "Me, too; I can't wait." Said Colleen. "What are your plans afterwards, Colleen?" "I'm thinking about taking some night classes at the community college, but I'm working with my aunt during the day." "Doing what?" "Companion for elderly." "You know how to do that?" "Yeah, I've been working with my aunt for a while now." Said Colleen. "What do you do?" Alvenia asked. "She works for an agency that sends her out to different homes to feed and bathe old people, and she cleaned their homes sometimes, too; I help her." "That doesn't sound bad." "It's not. My aunt's pay isn't bad, either. What's your plans, Alvenia?" Alvenia thought quickly and said, "I'm going to work at a hotel." "You're not going to college?" "Maybe later. There's the bell. I'll talk to you later, Colleen." "Alright girl!"

That evening, Jessica was late. "What took you so long?" "Just get in the car, Alvey. And please don't slam that door. I told you not to slam it!" "I didn't, the wind did it. Where have you been, Aunt Jessie?" "I took a co- worker somewhere; I thought she'd be done sooner." "It looks like it's going to storm out here: I thought I was going to get rained on." "It is a storm near the coast; so, we've got to secure the house. By the way, Alvey' you don't have to cook, I got some fried chicken and coleslaw from Pete's deli." "It smells good: I'm hungry, too." Said Alvenia. "Didn't you eat today?" "I had some chips." "Alvey!" Jessica said, loudly. "I told you I don't like eating in the cafeteria, Aunt Jessie." "You should, It's a free lunch, Alvey. You can make us a plate after we're done with everything."

When they got home, Jessica said, "I have a few calls to make: Close all the windows and bring in the pansies." "Can't we eat first; I'm starved." "I think it's best you take care of that first Alvey; It's up to you if you want to bring in your flowers later." "What's that on the porch?" Alvenia asked. "It looks like something the mail carrier left. Take that bag from the back seat." Jessica said, in a hurry.

When they stepped onto the porch, Jessica picked up the package and said, "Oh, these are some shoes I ordered." "I thought we didn't have extra money to shop with, Aunt Jessie." "Would you just go do what you supposed too, Alvey; please."

Alvenia put the bag on the kitchen table, then went out back and grabbed 3 pots of plants. She took them inside and set them on the kitchen floor. Afterwards, she grabbed a piece of chicken; She went in her room and ate it before she took her time to secure the house, and made Jessica a plate: She wanted her to wait.

A half hour later she heard," What's taking you so long Alvey?! Bring me my food!" "I'm in the bathroom! I'll be right there!" Alvenia said, shouting. Then she stood in the bathroom doing nothing, just to make Jessica wait longer. She came out after 10 minutes. "Here's your food." "It's about time."

Alvenia laughed so inside she could barely say: "Do you want something to drink?" "Bring me a coke. Better yet, make some tea." "Whatever you want, Aunt Jessie." While Alvenia made the tea, she thought," I'm so ready to leave here. Which reminds me, I need to call Mama Fran. Aunt Jessie's sleeping pills are in the medicine cabinet; I should put one in her tea to Knock her out for a while. Yeah, that's what I'll do. Why didn't I ever think of that?"

"Here's your tea, Aunt Jessie." "Can't you see I'm reading; Put it on the stand." "Alright I'll be in the kitchen if you need me." "Just go!" Jessica said, feeling agitated. Alvenia walked out and left the door partially open. A half hour later she went back to peek in on Jessica; she was asleep.

CHAPTER 7

Graduation Style

AFTER JESSICA WENT to sleep, Alvenia went in the kitchen and called, Francine. "Hello. Hellooo! I guess they hung up." Betty Lou said. Moments later Alvenia called again. Francine answered on the first ring. "Mama Fran?" "Yes." "Hi, it's Alvenia." "Hi Gloria, I'm getting changed for bed; call me back in a few minutes, Hon!" Francine hinted. Alvenia got the hint and said," Ok ma'am."

When she called back, Francine answered again. She said, "Hello Dear, did you get my hint when I called you, Gloria?" "Yes, Miss Betty was in there." "She was, but I was waiting for your call; how's everything?" "Everything is okay, ma'am." "Do you have everything you need?" "Like what ma'am?" "A new dress for one, so you'll be nice and pretty when you graduate: even though you're already pretty." "Thanks Mama Fran." Alvenia said, smiling. Francine went on and said," And your hair' are you going to the salon, or is Jessica going to do it?" "I doubt it." "Why do you doubt it, Cookie?" "Because she didn't have anything done to it for my senior pictures: not to mention (buy me a new dress) either." "She didn't?" "No, ma'am. She gave me one of hers, then suggested I wear my favorite shoes with it. Although I do like the shoes I plan to wear; They're a pair you gave. But I really don't think she's going to do anything to my hair, and her dresses are too big for me." "I'm sure they are. What your size?" "(5-7)." "I figured that; You're small like me." Alvenia grinned before she said, "Aunt Jessie's dresses are sizes (10-12)." "That's much too big for you. I'll tell you what, come on Saturday if you could; I might be able to work something out." "Okay ma'am, good night." "Good night, Sweetie'."

Jessica had the weekend off. That Saturday, she made Alvenia go with her on a fishing outing. So, Alvenia saw Francine the following Monday. She was there at 5:15 pm. "Yes!" "It's Cookie, ma'am!" "One moment Hon." Francine slowly stood up from her recliner, grabbed her walker, then went to the door. "Hi, come in and have a seat." Alvenia set in her recliner, she set in her rocker. "How are you today, Mama Fran?" "I'm feeling pretty good, Hon; how are you?" Alvenia scooted back in the recliner. She said, "I'm fine, just ready to leave here." "I know you are, Sweetie. Do you see that shopping bag over in the corner?" "Yes." "Go get it." Alvenia, got the bag and set back down. Francine then said, "Open it." Alvenia asked, "What is it, ma'am?" "Take a look." "This is a beautiful dress, Mama Fran." "I see you like it." Francine said, smiling." Alvenia said," I Love it." "Well it's yours Dear; You can wear it to your graduation, and to other occasions as well." "You didn't have to do this, Mama Fran." "I wanted too; You don't need to be wearing a (too big old dress) to your graduation." "Ma'am, this dress cost $149; when did you buy it?" "Last Friday." "Did Miss Betty take you?" "Nope." "I don't understand, ma'am." "Let's just say,' I have a couple of other sources I can call on every now and then; this one was a niece from my husband's side.' She called Macy's and had it delivered to me. Betty Lou thinks it's, mine. She fussed and told me I had enough dresses already, but I wasn't listening to that yapping. You want to know what else she said?" "What ma'am?" "This dress looks kinda young for you, I might want to wear it." I said: "No you're not either." (ha, ha, ha!) "Little does she know, that's your dress, Cookie." "Thank you". "You don't have to thank me, Dear." "Yes, I do. You're so kind. And I already have a place to hide it from, Aunt Jessie." Alvenia said, humbly. "Very good, Dear." Alvenia went on and said," I think I'll fold it neatly and put it in my backpack, then change into it before the ceremony begins." "That is a good idea, and don't forget, we're leaving the next day. So just pack your main necessities and I'll be by in a taxi to pick you up." "Alright, ma'am." "And we have to communicate up to then, Cookie." "Okay, I'll call you." "Good enough." Francine said, nodding her head." "I'm going to go now." "Are you walking around?" "No Ma'am. I'm going to jog back through the woods." "Alright, let yourself out and lock the door." "Bye!" "It's not bye Cookie, see you later." "See you later!" Alvenia said, smiling.

A wonderful week passed, and Alvenia's graduation day had come. She was up earlier and in great spirit. As that's how excited she was. Jessica entered the kitchen. "Something smell's good, but why are you making breakfast this early, Alvey?" "I'm hungry." "You're hungry?" "Yes." Said Alvenia. "But you're usually in bed this time." "I guess I'm happy about graduating."

Jessica grin before saying: "There's no guessing, you are happy. What Dress are you wearing?" "The green one." "I like that one, too." "Aunt Jessie, aren't you happy for me?" "Of course, I am: I won't have to get up so early." "Isn't that job 8 to 4?" "I ask her to change your shift: It's 9:30 a.m. to 3 p.m." "Why?" Alvenia asked. "Because I don't have to be to work until 4 pm. Put my breakfast in the oven: I'm going back to my room."

The graduation was held at (August Martin High). On their way, Jessica said," What do you need with the backpack, Alvey?" "You know I don't like wearing high heels, Aunt Jessie: I'm taking my sneakers to put on after the ceremony." "Alright, I'm going to drop you off, because I have to go by my job for something: I'll be there in time." "Okay."

Jessica's dress had a collar similar to the one Francine gave. After Alvenia got out, she rushed inside to the lady's room and changed. On the way to meet the rest of her class, she saw Colleen. "Hi, Colleen." "Hi Alvenia; are you ready?" "Yes, I've been ready." "Me, too. But for some reason, I'm nervous." "Don't be nervous Colleen, it's a very special moment in our lives; be happy." "Thanks, Alvenia."

It was a large class and the ceremony was beautiful. When Alvenia accepted her diploma, she saw Jessica stand up and clap. As she exited the stage, she heard a familiar voice in the front row of seats. She looked down and saw Francine standing in front of her wheelchair. Then for a moment, she forgot everything and went and gave Francine a hug. After they'd hugged, Jessica was ready to leave. On their way home she said, "I'm proud of you, Alvey. Were you surprised to see Betty Lou and her aunt?" "I didn't see, Miss Betty." "You didn't see her because she was probably somewhere smoking a cigarette; I don't know why she won't quit." Jessica said, shaking her head. Alvenia said, "I was very surprised when I saw Miss Francine." "When I told them, Betty Lou said she really wanted to come." "I'm glad she did. I meant I'm glad they did." "I think I'll watch a movie this evening, Alvey. Don't forget you start work on Monday; I'm going to take you on Saturday to pick up your uniform." Alvenia looked straight ahead and thought," This woman thinks I'm a foolish idiot. That job will be waiting, because I'm leaving here: I can't wait to get from around this selfish lady." "What are you thinking about, girl?" Jessica asked. "What?" Alvenia said, startling. "You were gone for a couple of minutes; did you hear anything I said?" "Yeah." "I hope so, because now is not the time to drift."

When they got home, Alvenia warmed up some leftovers. Jessica fussed, but Alvenia didn't pay her any attention. After they'd eaten, Jessica went in the den, turned on the tv, and flopped on the sofa. Alvenia cleaned the kitchen, then went to her room. After a while, she went to the den and peeked in on, Jessica: She was asleep. And so, she went back to the kitchen and called, Francine.

She whispered, "Thanks for coming to my graduation." "You're welcome, Sweetheart. Are you packed and ready to leave?" "Yes, ma'am." "Good." Francine said, happily. Ma'am, I'm going to call you tomorrow after Aunt Jessie leaves for work." "Alright, and you might want to leave her a note, Cookie: but that's up to you." "I thought about it, and I'm going to wait until I'm situated, then give her a call." "Alright Dear, get a good night's rest." "Good night." "Good night, Hon!"

CHAPTER 8

Up and Away!

ALVENIA SLEPT WELL after she'd talked to Francine. She was up at 6:30 a.m., made her bed, brushed her teeth, then went and made breakfast. At 8: a.m., Jessica entered the kitchen. After she'd set down, Alvenia gave her a cup of coffee. She took a sip, then said, "It really does feel good not having to take you to school, and now since you'll be working, we should be able to buy a new car." Alvenia didn't say anything. She gave her a plate with grits, eggs, and a few slices of Canadian bacon. Jessica went on and said, "You must've known I was hungry, but I've got to hurry: We were short on staff yesterday, and they asked me to come early today." Then she gobbled down her breakfast. Afterwards, she stood up and said, "My bathroom needs to be cleaned, and don't forget to water the plants." "Okay, I'll See you later. Bye!" Said Alvenia.

She stayed in the kitchen until the ragged sound of Jessica's rusting car engine was gone. After a moment, she said, "Forget this kitchen, those plants, and her filthy bathroom, I've got to call Mama Fran; but first I better pack my shoes and toothbrush." She began to move quickly. "Don't be nervous Alvenia, slow down. Why am I talking to myself? Okay, everything is packed: now I can call Mama Fran."

Alvenia called but didn't get an answer. She called again and Francine answered on the 2nd ring. "Good Morning, ma'am." "Hi, Cookie. Are you ready?" "Yes." "Alright Dear, look out for my taxi; I should be there shortly." Alvenia had 1 small suitcase, and a tote bag. Although she was a bit nervous, her mind was made up. Then she heard the hunk from a taxi. On her way out, she suddenly stopped at the door, then looked all around the living room. She grabbed her graduation picture and a few more photos that hung in the foil. "So long Aunt Jessie."

When she got to the taxi, the driver was standing by the trunk. "Ma'am, you can put your things back here." Alvenia gave him her things. Afterwards he said, "Sit in the back, ma'am." When Alvenia opened the door, Francine was sitting there smiling. After Alvenia got in, they laughed and tightly embraced. That's just how elated they were. "Are you ready to go?" Francine asked. "Yes, ma'am!" Alvenia said, happy to leave. Then the driver got in. "Where too, ma'am?" He asked. "(JFK) John F. Kennedy International Airport, please." Said Francine. As they were driving away, Alvenia noticed a lady was sitting in the front. Afterwards, she moved closer to Francine. Then she whispered, "Is she with you, Mama Fran?" "Who?" "That lady." "Why don't you ask her? Go on and ask her; She won't bite." Alvenia tapped the lady on the shoulder and said," Hello." "Hello, Alvenia." "Oh my! What are you doing here, Colleen?! Mama Fran?! Will somebody tell me what's going on?" Alvenia said, surprised. The other passenger was Colleen. She and Francine were so tickled about Alvenia's expression. Francine said, "We'll tell you after we board the airplane: be patient." Alvenia was excited, but had no clue as to what was going on.

When they got out at the airport, the girls tightly embraced with jumps of joy. Then just before they boarded the plane, Francine said," Alright girls, say good-bye to Bronx." "Bye Bronx!" They said, full of joy. Alvenia thought," Bye Aunt Jessie'." Then after they'd gotten situated, she said," So we're going to Washington DC?" Francine answered," Yes, and you're going to John C. Hopkins University." So am I, Alvenia." "You Colleen?!" "Yes." Said Colleen. That was another cheerful moment for Colleen and Alvenia. "Relax girls, I'll tell you everything after we're settled." Francine said, smiling.

They landed in Washington at 2:15 pm. Then a taxi took them down town to pick up a rental car. From there, Colleen drove them to the Hay-Adams Hotel. After they'd checked in and got comfortable, Francine ordered room service. Then while they ate chicken salad with Mexican enchiladas, and drank Pepsi, Francine explained everything. "Girls, I've wanted to leave 'New York' for a very long time. Alvenia, I've been in a situation similar to yours for many years. What I mean is, my niece has been very unkind to me since my husband died." "But why?" Colleen asked. Francine answered, "Among a lot of reasons; I think basically because I'm not her biological relative. "As sweet as you are, she should be ashamed of herself to treat you that way." "Thank you, Colleen, but she has no empathy; I don't think she's a shame of anything, and I don't let her ignorance bothers me." Alvenia suddenly said, "Wait, I don't mean to change the subject, but I'm still shocked about you two: how long have you known each other?"

"Colleen's grandmother and I go way back. We've been friends since high school, and even though I went to college and she got married and had a family, we stayed in contact with one another, and we're still friends. So, when you told me about Colleen', I already knew her: I didn't tell you because I'd already planned to leave and take her with me. Then after finding out about your situation, she and I had a talk, and we thought it was a good idea to take you with us." "That means you were in on this the whole time, Colleen." Alvenia said, looking very serious. "Yes, Alvenia." Colleen said. "So that's why you were talking to me?" "Well yes and no; I really do like you, Alvenia." "How could you do that to me, Colleen?!" "Alvenia wait!" Colleen said, desperately. "I got you! (ha, ha, ha)! "Don't do that, Alvenia; You really did get me." Alvenia became very emotional and stood up. She hugged them and said," I'm sorry Colleen. I really like you, too; both of you. I'm so glad to leave there. Thank you all so much." "You're welcome." Said Francine and Colleen. Then Francine said," Sit down, Hon. Do you remember that day you told me you were accepted at John C. Hopkins?" "Yes, ma'am." Alvenia answered, still very emotional, yet happy. "Well, the next day I pulled some strings for you. How were you able to do that, ma'am?" "Don't ask me how; I'm glad I was able to do it." "Thank you." "You're welcome, and Colleen is going, too." Francine said, smiling. "That's great! I can't believe all this is happening!" Alvenia said, very excited. "Believe it, Sweetie." Said Francine. "Who's going to take care of you while we're in school, ma'am?" Alvenia asked, stretching her eyes." You're going full time and Colleen is going at night, that way she can help me during the day: She's come to the house and helped me a few times." "Did you really, Colleen?" "Yes, I did." "She sure did. In fact, you just missed her one day." "You two are so sneaky." Said Alvenia. (they laugh) Alvenia then went on and asked," Where do we go from here?" "You sure don't mind asking questions." Said Francine. (they all laughed again). "That's a surprise for you and, Colleen." "She's telling the truth, Alvenia; I have no idea." "Don't worry, you two will find out in a couple of days. And until then, let's just enjoy this nice hotel." "Aunt Fran?" "Yes, Colleen?" Alvenia, interrupted and said," Colleen you called her, 'Aunt Fran'." "I know; She's been Aunt Fran to me awhile." "That's nice. I call her, 'Mama Fran'." "That's even nicer, Alvenia." Colleen said, smiling.

"What were you about to say, Colleen?" Francine asked. "Oh yeah, if I may ask, how were you able to do all this?" "It's kind of a long story." "I don't care." Colleen said, while stretching her eyes and slightly moving her head from side to side. "Me either; let us hear it." Said Alvenia. Francine said, "Alright then. My husband was biracial. His father was white, and of course his mother was black. He had 1 brother. They were their only children. But his father was married to a white woman. That marriage had two daughters. However, after my husband and his brother became big boys, their father made sure the siblings knew one another, and he and the older sister became very close. She had a daughter named Monica. That girl loved her Uncle Franklin. After he'd passed on, she kept in touch with me." "So, Monica is white?" "Yes, she's white, Cookie. Betty Lou never liked her, and that's why we always kept our conversations confidential. Monica is the one that helped me put all this together. She's here, also. "She is?" "Yes, Colleen; You two will get to meet her tomorrow. I'm sorry not tomorrow, I didn't mention, she was an on-call doctor." "WOW, a doctor!" Said Colleen. "Yes, and she'll be here the day after tomorrow: I assure you're going to like her." Said Francine.

Francine and the girls enjoyed their 2 day stay at Hay-Adam. The day they left she had, Alvenia to drive them to their location. Then after riding 10 minutes, they drove up to Francine's dream home. It had 3 floors, 4 bedrooms, and 3 bathrooms. Both Alvenia and Colleen were amazed about how beautiful it was. "Is this where we're going to live? They asked. "Yes, this is our home." Francine said, smiling from the abundance of happiness. When they went inside the girls were so stunned their jaws dropped. The inside was quaint with Victorian furnishing and accessories. Everybody had their own room and bath. Other amenities include a huge eat in kitchen, an elegant dining room for 10, a moderate size den with a brick fireplace, a small office, and a screened in patio with pool, and jacuzzi. It had a 3-car garage, also. They all were very excited.

That evening, Francine ordered Chinese food. After dinner, they went in the den and got comfortable. Then they talked. "Mama Fran, are you rich?" Alvenia asked. Francine answered, "I will not say I'm rich, but when my husband passed on, we were afloat enough for me to live comfortably. And all I ever wanted to do was live happy and help others. So, you see, I'm rich in heart, and here I am, ready to live as happy as I could, and in hope to make your lives happier." Colleen and Alvenia felt much gratitude. They said, "Thanks, we love you!"

Later that night, Colleen called her family. They wished her well. The next day, Francine called Betty Lou. She asked Francine where she was. Francine said," Never mind where I'm at, I'm fine. I called to tell you, you can have that car, but you've got 60 days to get out of that house: It's been sold." Betty Lou, fussed. Francine said bye and hung up. The next day, Betty Lou went and spoke with Francine's bank. Her financial adviser said she'd transferred all her accounts with confidential access. Betty Lou then argued with the adviser and was escorted out by the bank's security. That same day, Alvenia and Colleen were elated to Meet Monica: They liked her a lot.

Alvenia, did leave her Aunt Jessica a note: She left it on the kitchen table. Jessica saw it the night, Alvenia left. It read," Dear Aunt Jessie, I'm a young lady now and I've moved on. Don't ever doubt or think I don't appreciate what you did for me, because I do. For 13 years you gave me a place to live, but you treated me badly: Not to mention I never felt loved by you. But I still love you, that's why I moved on. Now you can have the life you deserve and take care of yourself for a change, and maybe someday you'll mature like I did. By the way, don't worry about me, I'm fine. And until we speak again, take care of yourself. Alvenia"

THE END

EPILOGUE

AFTER 6 YEARS, Francine and the girls still lived together. Colleen, often spoke with her family. She graduated with a (Business Degree) and became (CEO of a Cleaning Service). Later, she married a (ENT Physician) Ear, Nose, and Throat, Doctor: He was Italian. 2 years later, they had a daughter and named her, Sierra. Alvenia, obtained a degree in Journalism and became an anchor for (NBC News Network). She was dating a black Professional NBA Player, also. Mrs. Francine Nesbit was doing pool therapy twice a week, and was living happier than ever. She never told Betty Lou, Colleen, or Alvenia about 1.5 million dollars she and her husband received from the company who was liable for their injuries. And she and Alvenia never looked back at, Betty Lou, Jessica, or The Bronx.

ABOUT THE AUTHOR

SOPHIA GAYLE D. EUTSEY is phenomenal. She's an astute formal General Clerk and Caregiver, a people person but put God and Christ first. She likes to read and write, also.

Her Quote: It's not about how many books I write, It's the richness of every story.

Printed in the United States
By Bookmasters

———